Peter Abbitt and the Big Flood

Peter Abbitt
and the Big Flood

Kathy Young

Illustrations By
Lyndsey Morris

NEW YORK

LONDON • NASHVILLE • MELBOURNE • VANCOUVER

Peter Abbitt and the Big Flood

© 2023 Kathy Young

Published in New York, New York, by Morgan James Publishing. Morgan James is a trademark of Morgan James, LLC. www.MorganJamesPublishing.com

Proudly distributed by Ingram Publisher Services.

A **FREE** ebook edition is available for you
or a friend with the purchase of this print book.

CLEARLY SIGN YOUR NAME ABOVE

Instructions to claim your free ebook edition:
1. Visit MorganJamesBOGO.com
2. Sign your name CLEARLY in the space above
3. Complete the form and submit a photo
   of this entire page
4. You or your friend can download the ebook
   to your preferred device

ISBN 9781636980232 paperback
ISBN 9781636980249 ebook
Library of Congress Control Number:
2022943924

Cover and Interior Design by:
Chris Treccani
www.3dogcreative.net

Illustrated by:
Lyndsey Morris

Morgan James is a proud partner of Habitat for Humanity Peninsula
and Greater Williamsburg. Partners in building since 2006.

Get involved today! Visit MorganJamesPublishing.com/giving-back

This book is dedicated to C.D. Young, my late husband.
This book would not have been possible without
his unwavering love and support.

Once upon a winter many years ago, it snowed and snowed and snowed some more. At first, the children loved seeing the gentle snowflakes fall.

The boys and girls frolicked in the snow, played in the snow, sledded in the snow, made snow angels in the snow, and threw snowballs for hours as the snow fell.

It was also snowing over at Med—O—Farm, where Peter Abbitt, — the horse who thought he was a dog —lived. Peter came to the farm when he was just a young colt. Since he only had dogs for playmates, he learned to chase the farm cats by watching them run from the dogs. Now, Peter was older and liked to stay inside his barn wearing an old, warm, red and green plaid blanket over his back. He would eat the hay, oats, apples and carrots that Mr. Abbitt brought to him each day. Today he thought it was a little too snowy to go outside and look for a cat to chase. After a while, the snow stopped falling.

A few days later another snowstorm moved into the town and dumped many more inches of the freezing white stuff. This happened so many times over the winter that people stopped counting the storms and started wishing for spring. Even the children were tired of playing in the snow and were wishing to go back to school.

Then March came and eventually spring arrived with slightly warmer temperatures. The trees started budding out with their pink and white blossoms, and the yellow and purple crocuses popped up out of the ground. The ice in the mountain streams began to thaw, and water flowed down into the rivers below. Everyone was so happy to discover that spring was here. Children, their friends and families went outdoors to take walks and play in the sunshine.

Even Peter ventured out of his barn to nibble on the first tender pieces of green grass that grew in his pasture.

Unfortunately, the sunny days did not last very long. Dark clouds blew in and filled up with rain. It rained in the mornings. It rained in the afternoons. It rained in the evenings and into the nights. When boys and girls went to bed, it was raining. When they woke up, it was still raining. Everyone wore raincoats and rain boots every time they went outside. Peoples' yards filled up with rainwater, and the ditches filled up with muddy water because the rain had no place to drain.

The rivers were already so full of snow melt that soon the water spilled over into the roads. Cars were getting flooded and becoming stuck in the waves on the streets. School was canceled because the big yellow buses could not drive in the muddy streams flowing down the middle of the roads.

The rivers flooded so fast and so high that muddy swirling rainwater flowed right below the surface of the bridge. Police officers came and placed barricades at the ends of the bridge so that the town folks knew not to try to drive their cars or trucks or wagons over it.

The families on the other side of the river could not drive over to town to get their groceries. Mothers and fathers started running out of food. Children did not have yogurt or cheese to eat. Boys and girls did not have any milk to drink or pour on their cereal. The river showed no signs of receding or going down.

Mothers and fathers started calling the dairy farm where Mr. Abbitt used to work before he retired. They begged him to find a way to bring them food. Mr. Abbitt felt sorry for the families, but he did not know how to help them.

Perplexed, Mr. Abbitt wondered what he could do to help his friends and longtime customers. Eventually, he remembered the old wooden wagon that he had used for so many years to deliver milk to neighborhood families. Wood is buoyant, which means it will float, so if the flood water became too deep, the wagon would float right through it. Now he just needed someone strong and brave to pull the wagon. Suddenly, he had an idea of who that just might be.

Peter Abbitt stayed inside his stall in his barn, thankful that he was warm and dry. Even the dogs, puppies, cats and kittens stayed in the barn keeping dry. They all had to remain in the barn for so long that they became very lazy. There was nothing to do. Dogs did not chase cats, and cats did not chase mice. Everyone was so bored. They were very lucky that Mr. Abbitt came every day to feed them and bring fresh water.

One day, Mr. Abbitt came to the barn and went over to the old wooden wagon to check it out. He wanted to see if it was in good enough condition to use to transport milk, cheese, and yogurt to families that needed food. Peter perked up his ears when he heard Mr. Abbitt banging on the wagon with a hammer to repair the broken boards.

Even the dogs and cats woke up long enough to stare Mr. Abbitt's way and wonder why he was making so much noise.

The next morning dark and early, Mr. Abbitt came back and went over to Peter and started whispering in his big old ear. "Come on Peter. I need you to help me help some folks who need food. I know I promised you that you could quit working and not pull that clunky old wagon, but this is a serious situation. Please. Peter. let me hook you up and let's get going. Peter looked into Mr. Abbitt's kind eyes and lowered his head so he could slip the bridle over his head.

Mr. Abbitt remembered to place the straw hat with the flower on it over his long ears to help keep his head dry. Mr. Abbitt led Peter outside and hooked him up to the wagon.

Some men from the dairy loaded the wagon with milk bottles, boxes of cheese, cottage cheese, butter and yogurt. It was still raining, and the long road to town was very muddy. Peter had to walk slowly so he did not slip and cause the wagon to shift and turn over. It took a long time for Mr. Abbitt and Peter to make their way down to the swollen riverbanks.

At one point, the water was flowing so fast down the street that the wagon started floating. Mr. Abbitt became very nervous that the wagon would float into a tree or a fence and become stuck. Peter could feel the icy water rushing past his legs and under his belly. He felt a little nervous, too. Would the water become deeper? Would the water become so deep that his feet would not touch the ground? Would he have to start swimming and worry that the wagon would pull him into a dangerous spot?

The bridge to the other side of the river soon came into view.
The river was starting to spill over the roadway onto the bridge.

Peter and Mr. Abbitt pulled up to the edge of the bridge. Mr. Abbitt yelled, "Whoa, Peter!" He climbed off the wagon's seat and picked up the barricade to move it out of the way. When Mr. Abbitt climbed back up, he picked up the reins and said, "Giddy—up!" Peter looked through the raindrops and did not like what he saw. Peter did not move. Again, Mr. Abbitt said, a little louder, "Giddy—up!" Peter still did not move. He shook his big head as if to tell Mr. Abbitt that he did not want to cross the scary flooded bridge. What if the wagon and Peter and Mr. Abbitt were swept off the bridge and into the angry churning river?

Just then, while Peter was struggling to make up his mind on whether to cross, a scrawny, very wet, gray kitten walked up to the other side of the bridge. The poor little kitty started meowing as if to say, "I'm shivering and hungry and so tired of being soaked to the skin, and I need someone to take care of me!"

Peter perked up his very large ears upon hearing the cat's cry. He raised his ears, quickly lowered his head, gave a little snort, and began to move in the cat's direction. He really loved to chase cats, and it had been a long time since he had been able to get out and run. First, the old horse walked slowly. Then he trotted and splished and splashed through the river water. Finally, he moved so fast that he very quickly reached the other side of the river. All Mr. Abbitt could do was hold on to the reins for dear life.

When Peter approached the dripping kitten, he came to a complete stop. The little guy did not run away. Peter was confused. Why was this cat still sitting and not running away? The kitten was so young that he had never been chased before and never thought he might be in danger. Peter lowered his big head and gently sniffed the gray kitty and wondered why he was able to get so close to a cat. This never happened to him before.

Mr. Abbitt knew he had to get Peter to continue his way to deliver milk, but Peter was not going to ignore this cat. So, Mr. Abbitt had another great idea. He climbed down from the wagon, picked up the kitty, and put him gently inside his fleecy rain jacket to keep him warm. The soggy kitty finally felt toastier than he had in many days and quickly snuggled down against Mr. Abbitt's warm body. Now Peter was ready to move ahead.

Mr. Abbitt clambered back up on the wagon and shook the reins and said, "Giddy up." Peter knew what he had to do and moved forward up the first street. Mr. Abbitt hollered out to the houses they passed, "Milk, cheese, yogurt!"

One by one, the front doors opened, and mothers and fathers and children came out to the wagon. The families were so happy to be able to have the food that they shook Mr. Abbitt's hand and patted him on the back for being so brave. Peter leaned down so people could pat him on his head and scratch him behind his long, wet ears. One little girl even brought out a big orange carrot for Peter to munch on. He was very hungry from pulling the wagon so far. Plus, Peter really enjoyed the attention. He did not understand that he and Mr. Abbitt were heroes for risking their lives to help their neighbors.

As people were gathering out in the street, a strange thing happened. The rain stopped, the clouds parted, the sun came out, and a colorful rainbow appeared in the sky. A beautiful sound was heard as everyone started cheering that the storm was finally over. Then an even more wonderful sound was heard as people sang "For He's a Jolly Good Fellow" to Mr. Abbitt. Normally a shy fellow, Mr. Abbitt was heard to say, "Aw shucks. I was glad to do it. It was Peter who did all the hard work!" Peter looked up from chewing his carrot as if to say, "I was just glad to get out of that barn for a little while!"

Mr. Abbitt turned the now empty wagon around and started back to the bridge. The river had started to recede, so the bridge was much easier to cross. Mr. Abbitt felt something moving inside his jacket. He unzipped it just enough to see a little kitty head poke out and use its pink nose to smell the fresh clean air. Mr. Abbitt smiled and rubbed the kitten's soft fur. He thought to himself that since the kitty was the one who got Peter to cross that bridge, he certainly deserved to be given a good home. He said aloud, "Welcome to the family. Peter and I are going to call you Stormy"!

Stormy and Peter Abbitt, the horse who thought he was a dog, became the very best of friends. Folks often saw little Stormy riding on Peter's back while clinging to the long hair of Peter's mane as they wandered the farmyard and pasture during the daylight hours.

Every night they shared a nice, warm,
comfortable stall in Mr. Abbitt's barn.

THE END

About the Author

Kathy Young worked 38 years in elementary education as a first and second grade teacher. She also served as a certified reading specialist who understood the need for quality literature that not only entertained children, but also educated them. Her first book – *Peter Abbitt, the Horse Who Thought He Was a Dog* – was based on a story her father created to delight Kathy and her sister at bedtime. The second book continues the adventures of Peter. Kathy currently resides in Virginia with her dog, Lola.

About the Illustrator

Lyndsey Morris has felt and expressed a true artistic passion for as long as she can remember. Her grandmother saw the natural talent and enrolled Lyndsey in private art lessons as a child to encourage and cultivate that innate talent. Lyndsey has combined her formal lessons with her natural talent to bring text to life in this work and more.

A free ebook edition is available with the purchase of this book.

To claim your free ebook edition:

1. Visit MorganJamesBOGO.com
2. Sign your name CLEARLY in the space
3. Complete the form and submit a photo of the entire copyright page
4. You or your friend can download the ebook to your preferred device

M·J Morgan James
BOGO™

A **FREE** ebook edition is available for you or a friend with the purchase of this print book.

CLEARLY SIGN YOUR NAME ABOVE

Instructions to claim your free ebook edition:
1. Visit MorganJamesBOGO.com
2. Sign your name CLEARLY in the space above
3. Complete the form and submit a photo of this entire page
4. You or your friend can download the ebook to your preferred device

Print & Digital Together Forever.

Snap a photo

Free ebook

Read anywhere